MW00904316
Nay Nay Oma Mo
Sobo Granny Gra
Abuelita Chichi Nonnie Momo
Biba Nyanga GeeGee NaNa
Nonna Momo Mummi
Mummo Gramms
GeeGee Mummo
Abuelita
Bibi Gigi Oma
Momo Chichi Nay Nay
Bibi
Grandmum Biba
Nyanga Nonnie Nyanga
Babooshka NaNa Nonna
Baba Mummi Grammee Gigi NaNa
Gramms Baba Sobo Momo Chichi
#1 GRAN

CLOVE PUBLICATIONS, INC.
Here There Everywhere

Library of Congress Cataloging-in-Publication Data
When Did I Meet You Grandma? written by Justin Matott; illustrated by Laurie McAdam - 1st ed. p. cm.
Summary: A child asks the question; "When Did I Meet You Grandma?" and remembers their occasions together.
ISBN 1-889191-11-6 {1. Old age–Fiction. 2. Grandparents–Fiction}
I. Laurie McAdam 1955– ill. II. Title

First edition A B C D E
Printed in Hong Kong

If you're interested in contacting Matott, please write to Clove Publications, Inc. or email him at RandomWrtr@aol.com
For Ms. McAdam please email Lauriemcadam@hotmail.com

With unlimited affection for:
Maribeth "NayNay" Harris, Grandma Bessie Allison and Grandma Maxine Ochoa. And in loving memory of Julia "Oma" Matott, Anne "Nana" Engle and Elizabeth "Nana" Harris
–JM

For:

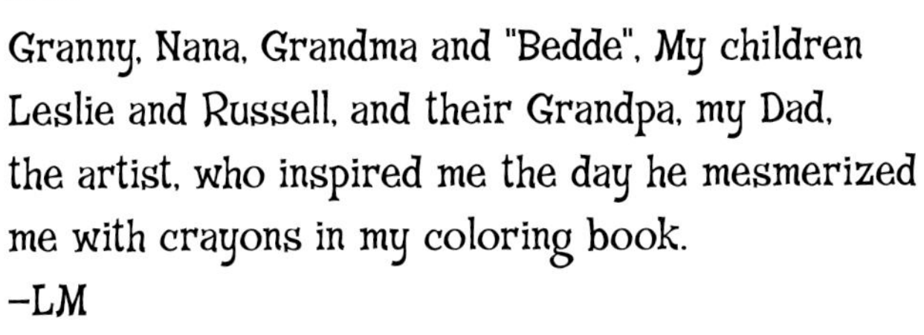

Granny, Nana, Grandma and "Bedde", My children Leslie and Russell, and their Grandpa, my Dad, the artist, who inspired me the day he mesmerized me with crayons in my coloring book.
–LM

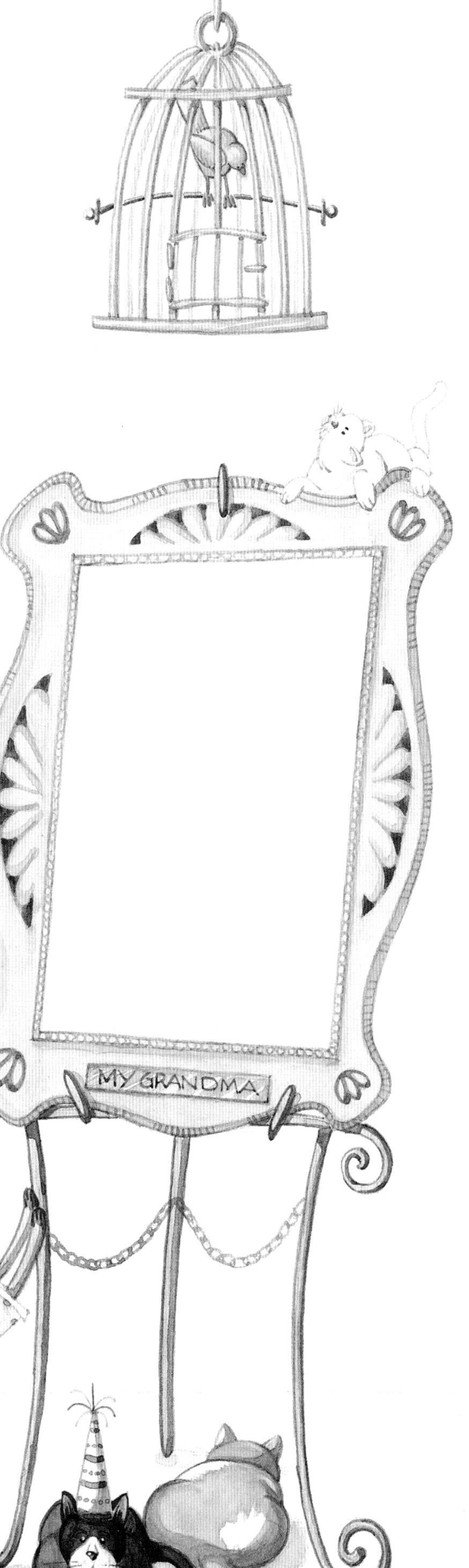

When did I meet you grandma? Seems I've known you all along!
You tell me funny stories; we sing your favorite song.

I remember when you sang to me, when I was in my bed.
Or maybe I imagined this, but that's what's in my head.
You have a different way 'bout you; treat me special and real nice.
You always seem to listen, even if I've told you twice.

I've looked at all your photos,
when you still looked brand new,

but, I like the way you look today,
and all the things you do.

Your skin is soft and wobbly, it gathers 'round your chin,
and I can see my Mommy's face, those times I make you grin.

I hear your bones all creaky; maybe it's just the stair?
When you are too tired to play, we read two in a chair.

U.F.O.
SPACE MONSTERS

You read to me at bedtime,

you don't mind it when I wiggle.

And when you use the monster voice,

you always make me giggle!

You tell me all your memories, of times so long ago.
What happened long before me, without you, I wouldn't know.
It's fun to hear the stories, of when Mommy was a child.
Compared to her activities, the things I do seem mild!

You tell me about Daddy, when he was just a kid.
When he got into mischief and all those things he did.

When you're coming for the holidays,
excited I do feel!
I share with you all my secrets,
while we prepare a meal.

We sew and bake, make jams and stuff.
"Folks are too busy now," you've said.

You will teach me all those things,
"There's lots of room in my young head."

We plant things in the garden, "I always have", you say,
"We used to grow all sorts of things, back in my younger day."

You never seem to sweat the stuff
that bothers mom and dad.

I scream and laugh and run around,
you never get too mad.

I hope some day to have grandkids, I'll be just like you are.
I'll let them eat their crumbly stuff, when they are in my car.

Mom never lets me eat the things, which you say are just fine.
We like to snack on the same things, we think they are divine.

Daddy raises his eyebrow,

when he sees my candy pile.

And though he likes to grumble,

I see his little smile.

You have a unique place and role,
spoiling me is your right!
"So do I have to eat the rest?"
"Well, maybe just one bite."

Yes, you are a special person. In my life you hold a place!

Someday when I look at myself,

I'll see some of your face.

Perhaps one day you'll live with us.

Tea parties just for three.

While you sit at the table,

I will climb the backyard tree.

And when you're gone, I will be sad. I'll wish you were still here.
Yes, in my heart you'll always be. It's you I will hold dear.

But that day is a long way off.
We have so much to do!
There are so many things right now,
I need to learn from you!

When I see all that we have done, my face gets such a smile.

We have so many memories, all in our photo file!

a kitty for Grandma
CHRISTMAS
new sweater knitted by Grandma... and my goofy brother!
Photos
HI!

Enough of all these stories! Let's get busy doing stuff.
We'll cherish all our moments; no time could be enough.
We've places to go and people to see, adventures yet to do!
Yes grandma, I'd go anywhere, as long as I'm with you!
So I'll ask you one more time, and sing your favorite song...
When did I meet you grandma? Seems I've known you all along...
ZOO

My Own Grandma

I call my Grandma Gramma

My favorite thing about my Grandma is when u spend the night at her house.

My Grandma is wonderful because she's fun

I love it when my Grandma and I play together

My favorite memory of my Grandma is

I love my Grandma because she's special.

Grandmas are different from parents because we do things that they don't always let us do.

My funniest memory of my Grandma is

My favorite book to read with Grandma is any book